HIDDEN PICTURE PUZZLE
Coloring Book

Anna Pomaska

Dover Publications, Inc.
New York

Hidden Picture Puzzle Coloring Book is a new work, first
published by Dover Publications, Inc., in 1980.

International Standard Book Number

ISBN-13: 978-0-486-23909-5
ISBN-10: 0-486-23909-8

Manufactured in the United States by Courier Corporation
23909826   2014
www.doverpublications.com

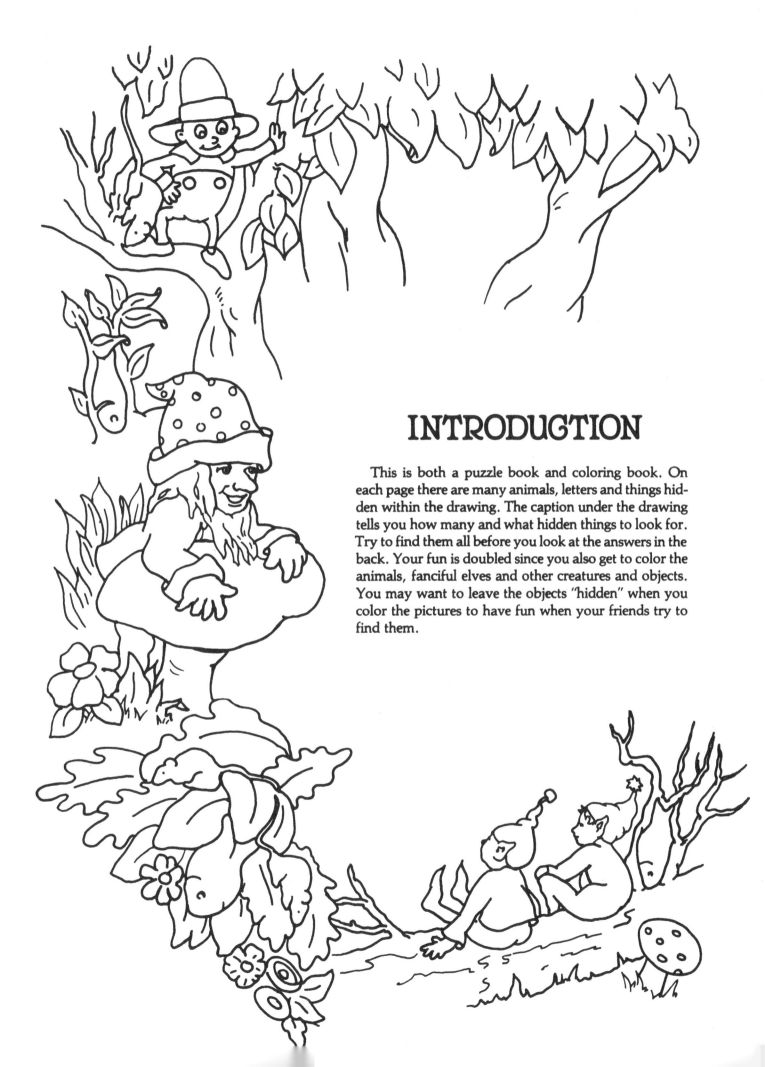

INTRODUCTION

This is both a puzzle book and coloring book. On each page there are many animals, letters and things hidden within the drawing. The caption under the drawing tells you how many and what hidden things to look for. Try to find them all before you look at the answers in the back. Your fun is doubled since you also get to color the animals, fanciful elves and other creatures and objects. You may want to leave the objects "hidden" when you color the pictures to have fun when your friends try to find them.

The turtle is looking for the fish pond and mouse house, but has lost his way. Some friendly dwarves tell him that if he could only find some fish or mice, they would surely tell him the way. Help turtle find the **9 fish** and **5 mice** hidden in the picture.

On his way to the fish pond, turtle first stops to visit the mouse house in Fairy Glen. He can see only three mice at home, but he knows there are others scampering about. Can you find the other **9 mice** and **5 fish** in this picture?

The old trees are sadly telling the wood imp that all their beautiful birds have disappeared. The wood imp laughs at this news because he and the frogs and fish know the birds are playing a springtime joke on the trees and have hidden themselves. There are **21 birds** in the picture. Can you find them?

The imp and elves all wish to have a bird to ride, but the woodland birds are playing their favorite game of hide and seek. In this picture you will find **11 birds, 3 elf slippers** and **1 pointed elf hat with a round tassel on top.**

These elves have found a very lively bird to ride, and are now having trouble keeping their slippers, socks and hats with all the bouncing. Can you find their lost things? There are **5 elf slippers, 5 pointed elf hats, 2 socks and 2 birds** hidden here.

When wood imps and fairies are happy, they say, "We feel dancey." The wood imps in this picture are feeling very dancey indeed. They are celebrating the arrival of the May flowers brought by the flower

fairies. The woodland rabbits are also feeling dancey, but are dancing so quickly it is difficult to see them. Can you find the **20 rabbits** in this picture?

The clouds that give April showers are waving goodbye. Four laughing leprechauns with pointed hats have hidden 4 pots of gold to celebrate the rainbow's arrival. Can you find the **4 laughing faces** and the **4 pots of gold**?

These elf children are having a magical flight with their bird friend. Hidden in the picture are other things, some of which can also fly. Find **1 airplane, 1 elephant's head, 1 heart, 1 kite, 1 flag, 1 horse's head, 1 sheep's head, 1 bat, 1 envelope** and **1 ice cream cone.**

The mischievous March wind has caught up many different items in its breezy travels. Can you find all the things that are whirling and tumbling about him? There are **2 dresses, 2 socks, 1 shoe, 1 cap, 1 umbrella, 1 spoon, 1 broom** and **1 sailboat.**

The toy bear and little elf have been given an airplane. Now they can play in the air with the winged fairy children. Many numbers are also joining the flying fun. Hidden in the picture are 0, 2, two 3's, 4, 5, 6, 7, two 8's, 9 and 10.

All the birds have gathered together to seek wisdom from the fabulous simurgh, a very ancient and wise bird told about in Persian tales. Here we see the simurgh telling the birds that there are hidden

things around them and that to be wise they must look carefully for **five 2's, two 3's, two 4's, three 5's, five 6's, four 7's, two 8's,** and **one 9.** There are 24 numbers in all.

The frogs are having such a wonderful time in the pond, they have forgotten to look for their favorite things to eat. All around them you will find **2 dragonflies**, **8 butterflies**, **1 caterpillar** and **1 water bug**.

The water nymph is quietly watching the things in the pond. Besides the frog, she sees **6 butterflies**, **4 water bugs**, **1 snail** and **1 bird**. Do you see them too?

It is the rabbit's birthday. Everyone is having a wonderful time, including the hidden guest. Find the **big laughing rooster**, as well as **4 pointed party hats** just like the owl's, **2 crown party hats** like the pig's, and **4 pieces of cake** like that held by the rabbit.

The 3 mice are somewhat upset. They have come home for a supper party only to find all their good food has disappeared! But if they look very carefully, they will find **3 peanuts, 2 pies, 2 cheeses, 2 carrots, 2 beets, 2 walnuts** and **1 acorn.**

It is Halloween night and all the witches, ghouls and jack-o'-lanterns have come out to celebrate. The ghosts too are flying about, but true to their nature, have vanished into the night. Can you make them appear again? There are **16 ghosts** in the picture.

The greedy witch is very angry! All 10 of her pointed witch hats have been hidden by a playful goblin who has now disappeared. Find the **laughing face of the goblin** (but don't tell the witch where he is!) and the **10 witch hats**.

23

All the animals of the plain have hidden from the fearful-looking dragon, thinking that he might eat them. The dragon, however, is a good-hearted creature and only eats fruit. Pears are his favor-

ite. In the picture you will find the **dragon's heart, his bowl, cup, teapot, fork, knife, spoon** and **pear.** You will also find **3 elephants' heads, 2 lizards, 2 snails** and **1 chicken** that have hidden.

These two African masks were used for different purposes in the tribes in which they were made. One was used to scare away evil spirits and the other was used to bring good luck. If you search carefully, you will find two A's, three C's, two D's, four H's, three W's, three V's, two U's, two X's, two Z's, and one each of a, B, J, m, N, o, P, T and Y. They may be upside down or sideways, but not backwards.

Here we see an African dancer proudly wearing a very elaborate wooden mask he has carved. Hidden in the picture are **two A's, three C's, three L's, three V's, three X's** and **one** each of **D, d, E, F, f, H, J, S, U** and **W**. There are 24 letters in all. They may be upside down or sideways, but not backwards.

This is the beautiful goddess Galatea, riding across the ocean waves. Hidden around Galatea, her water chariot, the playful Cupids and strange mermen, are many objects and creatures from the sea

and elsewhere. Looking carefully you will find **3 hearts, 3 shells, 2 fish, 1 candle, 1 seal, 1 lizard, 1 bear's head, 1 pig's head, 1 angel, 1 bird, 1 snail** and **1 mermaid.**

These Indians believe that every action well done deserves a feather for remembrance. In this picture there are **23 feathers**! Color them in as you find them.

These are different Indian masks, and within each there are many hidden arrows. Can you find all **29 arrows** on the page?

The circus is in town and the parade has begun! Here is the big mother elephant, Mumbo, and her little baby, Gumbo. But there are **2 more elephants** hidden away in this picture as well as **2 seals, 2 apples, 2 horns, 1 heart, 1 sailboat** and **1 circus tent**. Can you find them?

The monkey and pig are having fun dancing around the stately camel and its happy rider. Look carefully to find 10 more animals and things that have joined the circus antics. There are **4 seals, 1 elephant, 1 turtle, 1 pig, 1 swan, 1 car** and **1 ice cream cone.**

Here are the Prince and Princess of Spring. Hidden around the Prince and his horse are **2 lizards**, **2 candles**, **1 eagle's head**, **1 shell**, **1 paintbrush**, **1 seal** and **1 bear**. Hidden around the Princess and her chariot are **2 angels**, **2 shells**, **1 whale**, **1 fish**, **1 lizard**, **1 feather**, **1 dress** and **1 heart**.

Sara is learning to read and doesn't realize that some of the letters from her book have danced out into the playroom. In Sara's picture find the letters A, F, P, E, H, T, D, U, S, t, v, e, n and o—one of each.

Sara's brother Angus is in the room playing with his locomotive. He too has not noticed the dancing letters around him. Can you see them? The letters are **F, B, A, J, C, L, w, h, j, u, n** and **k** (one of each) and **two O's**.

This is a picture of farm children riding their beloved cows. Besides the yard animals, we can clearly see there are several other hidden animals and things. There are **2 candles, 2 chicks, 2 rabbits, 1 horn, 1 pig, 1 mouse** and **1 squirrel.**

SOLUTIONS

page 4

page 5

pages 6 and 7

page 8

page 9

pages 10 and 11

page 12

page 13

page 14

page 15

pages 16 and 17

page 18

page 19

page 20

page 21

page 22

page 23

43

pages 24 and 25

page 26

page 27

pages 28 and 29

page 30

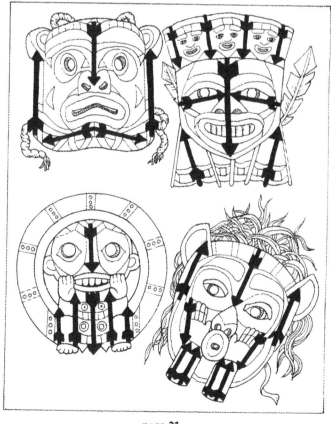

page 31

page 32

page 33

pages 34 and 35

page 36

page 37

page 38